Secret Life of a Dominatrix

Summer Bradford

Published by Summer Bradford, 2023.

SECRET LIFE OF A DOMINATRIX

First edition. July 17, 2023.

Copyright © 2023 Summer Bradford.

ISBN: 979-8223527428

Written by Summer Bradford.

Table of Contents

SECERT LIFE OF A DOMINATRIX
Mistress Trix

"What have you been up to lately? We hardly see you now" Tori asked.

How could I tell her what I have been up to? I knew she wouldn't understand about the world I was involved in when I left the gates of the university every day.

"Just studying, you know how it is" I replied.

I knew she didn't believe me, but I wasn't going to tell her what I did, even if she was one of my closest friends.

The truth was by day I was a student in my last year of university who hoped to be accepted into business law, but at night I hid a dark secret.

It started with a funny comment from one of my friends which had planted a seed in my mind that wouldn't go away.

The more I visualised myself wearing a tight leather dress with a whip in my hand, the more I knew I had to fulfill this new desire.

Keeping this secret life hidden from everyone around me was hard to do, but if they found out who I really was then they might try to make me stop, which I knew I couldn't.

There was also Mitch, handsome law student and athletic jock. Would he ever see who I really am, not just the girl behind the books and high grades?

Or could it be Max? Manager at my place of work. Dark, handsome and much older than the boys at school. Max gives me butterflies whenever he looks at me and I feel sexy and alive with excitement when he is near.

With a secret life, a crush on the University playboy and the overriding lust I feel for my manager at work, I feel torn in the choices I must make.

My name is Sarah Fielder, normal looking University student.

However, you may know me by my other persona, Miss Trix. Mistress Trix, Dominatrix.

Chapter 1

My whole life had been planned out by my parents since the day I was born.

They had chosen what I would study at Yale, where I would work afterwards and whom I might marry that would offer me the same lifestyle that they were accustomed to. Of course, my opinion was never a part of the equation and if I tried to tell them what I wanted to do with my life, it was usually dismissed immediately.

My family came from a long line of family inherited money and my parents owned over a thousand hotels throughout the world. Money was never an object to my parents, and I was lucky to be brought up without having to worry about it. Being wealthy came with other sacrifices though, such as being shipped off to boarding school at the age of five and never really seeing my parents. Don't get me wrong, I have travelled the world and seen things that most twenty-year-olds would never dream of, but travelling was always with a nanny who took care of me while my parents involved themselves in the social world of multi-millionaires.

At the age of 15, I begged my parents to take me out of boarding school and allow me to live at home so I could attend a regular school. I was desperately lonely, especially during spring break as my parents usually kept me in school because their business trips were important, and they had very little extra time to spend with me.

After weeks of relentless begging, they gave in, and I was able to stay at home under the supervision of our house staff. I was able to attend a public school in our neighbourhood, chosen by my parents, of course. It was a well-known school for children whose parents were wealthy and could afford the two-hundred-thousand-a-term fee. Not quite your run of the mill public school. Now that I was in university, my life was more my own.

I had been an A grade student at school with honours in business studies and I was now at Yale, undertaking a degree in business law. I knew my parents would be happy with this choice and it would be beneficial if I was ever to take over the family business.

My friends at school consisted of Tori; cheerleader-wannabe, future senators' wife, and Dale; fantastic pastry chef-wannabe, Gordon Ramsey's second wife. Two of my male best friends were fantastically gay, Chris and Jayden, and they loved each other fiercely and let everyone know it.

It was actually Jayden who made a comment one day that gave me the inspiration for the now secret life I kept from everyone.

On this particular day we were passing each other in the hallway, joking as we always did. I was wearing a tight black leather skirt that made a certain swooshing noise when I walked past. The skirt was below my knee, 1940's inspired and not really something I would normally wear.

I don't know why I chose to wear it that day, as I usually wore jeans, but this skirt made me feel sexy, and a little bit naughty. Sometimes, I just wanted to step away from the good girl, grade A student that everyone knew me to be, and today was one of those days.

When I walked past Jayden, he yelled out "Sarah, don't forget to collect the whip from my place honey, cause you look sexy baby-girl".

Now of course, Jayden was just being Jayden and this comment was nothing unusual for him as he was always calling people 'sexy' and referring to girls as 'baby-girl'. But the image of myself standing with a whip in my hand and a tight leather dress suddenly excited me.

When I arrived home that evening, I researched anything to do with whips, leather equipment and women dominatrix. The more I saw and read about it, the more I wanted to try it.

There was something completely forbidden and utterly sexy about having control over another human being. The fact that you were utterly desired by someone who wanted you to punish them, was interesting to me.

I was not interested in changing my outfits at school and becoming someone else in my day-to-day life. I just loved the idea of being something totally different outside of university and not the good girl that I was perceived to be at university.

With my heart racing, I rang a few places and each time I would hang up again. It took me four attempts to finally get the courage up to say hello and ask some questions.

When I ended the call, I decided to drive past the areas where these dominatrix establishments were located, which also helped me eliminate the ones I wouldn't work at.

One establishment stood out the most. The place was called 'Elite' and it was based in one of the wealthiest suburbs of L.A.

I rang them and talked to the manager, who was intrigued that I was going to university and was an honours student, yet was seeking out something different to experiment in. I couldn't blame him for being curious as there was something quite enticing about the good girl image wanting to do something very bad.

Meeting him and touring the rooms, I knew that I had found the place I wanted to work.

Every room was different, they had high standards of hygiene and the rooms were made to look like they were part of a luxurious five-star hotel, although this hotel had toys hidden in wall furnishings and secret cupboards. Not quite like the hotels my parents owned.

The excitement of knowing what went on in these rooms made my heartbeat faster and made my whole-body tingle. It was like liquid hot adrenaline rushing through my body, which completely turned me on.

I was offered the job on the spot and was given a card with the name of a clothing store on the back that I was instructed to visit before

I started work. I didn't need to ask questions about the money I would earn, as I knew it would well paid and I wasn't working for the money anyway.

There was something deep inside me that knew that I would be great at this.

This is where the persona of Miss Trix was born.

Miss Trix, Dominatrix.

Chapter 2

As the paddle came down swiftly and moved across his buttocks, I couldn't help but feel a sense of satisfaction and also just a little bit turned on.

"Do you like that? Do you like having your backside paddled?" I whispered in his ear.

"Yes, Miss Trix, please can I have more".

Standing in my tight latex catsuit with my thigh high boots and black leather masters mask on, I felt the kind of control that I had never known throughout my eighteen years.

I brought the paddle back and raised it higher then moved it down swiftly, leaving a nice red mark on his buttocks.

He cried out and I wondered if I had taken it a little bit too extreme, but we had a safe word and he was a regular client, so he could use it any time he wanted, though many of my clients never did.

I released the chains around his ankles and then untied his hands from the metal loops above the bed.

"Get up! Your time with Miss Trix is over, for today at least. You know where your clothes are stored, go and have a shower because you stink".

"Yes, Miss Trix. Thank you, Miss Trix".

I exited the room and then walked down the corridor passing rooms occupied by other Dominatrix's.

Max, the Manager of Elite, was in his office down the end of the corridor. I knocked on his door then opened it slightly.

"You wanted to see me, Max?"

"Yes Trix, come in and take a seat" he replied.

I walked in and sat down on the leather recliner. It was so comfortable and the squeak of the latex rubbing against the leather never failed to amuse me.

Max pointed to the trolley of alcohol by the side of the couch, but I shook my head signalling no.

"You know the rules Max, or at least you should as you're the one that issued them. No drinking on the job".

Max laughed.

"Sorry Trix, I almost forgot my own rules and that you still had a client waiting" he said, with a cheeky smile on his face.

"Well maybe when I'm not working, then I will accept that offer".

His gaze moved over my outfit, and I could see that he liked what he saw. What man wouldn't like seeing a woman in a latex outfit though? I'm sure it would be on most men's list to at least have that experience once in their life.

"You're good at what you do Trix, I will give you that. Most of your clients are regulars and you always keep it within the parameters of what we want to offer at Elite. I wonder if you would consider working more hours. I would be happy to increase your rate, plus you could get off punishing more clients".

He smiled and I realised that his good looks probably made many women weak at the knees.

"I can't work longer than I do now Max, as I have study for university. Plus, I also have the staff at home that report my coming and goings to my parents. Any suspicion that I'm doing something that I shouldn't mean me being shipped to Rome, and I would rather quit then let that happen".

"I think both you and I know that you quitting would never happen. You love what you do Trix, I can see it every time I watch you. It's a rare thing to have compassion for your customers but also have the thrill of inflicting pain on them. You're exactly what I need at Elite".

I looked at him and knew he was right. I wouldn't like to say I was obsessed with being a Dominatrix, it was more a desire that I had never been able to fulfil until now.

"Think about this then Trix. You have school break coming up soon and we have a planned special week-long event away from Elite. It's a retreat for wealthy clients with certain fantasies they wish to have carried out. Would you be interested?".

"It sounds like it could be fun, but I have to study for my exams".

"I will take care of that Trix. You can have all the time you need to study before seeing any clients. The money is great too, which could help you get your own place so you're not under the watchful eye of the house staff, or your parents".

"How much are you talking about?".

Max took a sip of his drink then placed it down on his desk. He lent forward with his elbows on the arms of his chair and his fingers laced together at his waist.

"Fifty thousand dollars for each customer".

My cat suit squeaked against the leather as I stood up and walked towards the door. I reached for the handle and then turned back around.

"Alright Max, I will accept your offer".

He gave me that gorgeous smile and my heart did summersaults as I walked out the door.

Chapter 3

"Sarah, your parents are returning for the weekend on Friday. Please don't arrange any outings with your friends as they have requested your presence here" Winston, our butler, instructed.

"Is there any reason why they're coming back? They're usually away in Monte Carlo at this time of the year".

"No miss, there was no indication why they're coming back, only that it was important for you to be here".

With that he turned and went back towards the main room. I grabbed the keys to my car and headed off to school.

I was very tired these past few days and the last thing that I needed was to have my parents' home to give me some news which probably only involved themselves.

Driving into the university carpark I saw Tori wave at me. I parked the car and walked towards her.

"What have you been up to lately? We've hardly seen you!" Tori asked, with a concerned look on her face.

How could I tell her what I have been up to? I knew she wouldn't understand about the world I was involved in when I left the gates every day.

"Just studying, you know how it is" I replied.

I knew she didn't believe me, but I wasn't going to tell her what I did, even if she was one of my closest friends.

"Well, Joe has a party planned at his holiday home in the Hamptons this weekend, can you come?"

"Unfortunately, not this weekend. My parents are flying in and have requested my presence" I said with a sarcastic tone.

"Really? That is how they put it? What do you think it's about?"

"I wouldn't have a clue, but I am guessing they have some long journey overseas planned that means they won't be home over vacation".

"Okay, so what will you do while they are away and you're off school?"

I had to think fast, as I knew I was going to be away at a retreat that I had promised Max I would work at.

"I may fly out and spend a couple of weeks wherever they are and get a tan. Or I might just stay at home and study, either way is fine by me. What about you, anything planned?" I asked, diverting the conversation quickly.

"We are heading to the Hamptons with the family and hopefully I will meet up with Joe while I'm there".

"Meet up? Don't you mean hook up with Joe while you are there" I replied, smiling and nudging her playfully with my elbow.

We both laughed, as we knew it was the truth. Tori had been hoping to get with Joe ever since she had biology class with him at junior high school. I couldn't blame her as he was very tall, a basketball pro and most of the girls at university thought he was ultra-good looking. He's not really my type, but Tori went for that whole sports-jock thing.

As we walked to our classes I couldn't help but look over at Mitch Bradley. Tall, brown eyes, black hair and the most gorgeous smile with pearly white teeth, he certainly was my type. When people talk about having a physical reaction to someone, call it chemistry if you like, well I had an unfathomable amount when I saw him.

Mitch wasn't your typical bad boy stereo type. He was one of the most academically gifted students at university, but he had that wild side look that a lot of girls were drawn to.

Yes, I lusted after him and it was chronic.

Chris and Jayden came up behind me and Jayden put his arms around me.

"Girl, you have to stop drooling after Mitch Bradley or you're going to have to wipe that drool away quickly before he sees it and discovers you have the hots for him".

I playfully jab him in the ribs, so he released me, and we walked into class.

He was right. If I didn't stop walking past him and practically dropping my panties every time I saw him, then one day he would discover my secret crush and the rejection would be so embarrassing!

A thought did cross my mind though. I wondered if Mitch Bradley would like to get chained up and whipped by Miss Trix?

It was an exciting thought to have.

Chapter 4

Dressing up as Miss Trix was always exciting.

After visiting 'lié dans les chaînes', the exclusive and private boutique store for all dominatrix clothing and specialty equipment, I'd discovered a way to create the persona of Miss Trix.

I picked out sleek cut wigs, latex dresses, cat suits, clinging tops, figure hugging skirts, thigh high boots, lace up stilettos, gloves and masks that, I felt, fitted my Miss Trix personality.

Putting on the outfits allowed me to morph into a different person. Miss Trix was confident, assertive, demanding and not to mention, sizzling hot!

It was the total opposite of what I felt like when I was at university. I was more of the jeans and baggy top, sneakers and ordinary reddish-brown hair. I didn't stand out; I was the boring looking brainiac.

However, as Miss Trix I could turn heads as soon as I walked into a room full of customers. I felt powerful and sexy.

I had chained my customer to the play rack, and I could already sense his excitement. The play rack had chains attached to the wall, so he was standing with his arms out to the sides and had his legs open wide, which were also secured with other chains. Most of my clients changed into their own special outfits but this particular client was a multi-millionaire businessman who liked to be chained and whipped while wearing his business suits. When I first met him, he told me he had total control over his company, employees and family, but when he came to Miss Trix, he wanted the control to be in my hands.

I had no issues with that!

I used the long whip against his back, and he screamed out in ecstasy. I couldn't help but wonder what he did with the suits afterwards and how he explained to his family that he always had to change them before coming home. You see, with the long whip it can cut, and I don't use it on many customers, but this particular customer requested it every time. He seemed to like the feel of the fabric cutting closely against his skin with each flick of the whip.

The whip slashed his business jacket to shreds and he stood there practically hanging from the arm chains exhausted and sweaty.

"Now, you're going to stay in this position for the next ten minutes while I leave the room. If you are good, then I will give you one more slash of the whip before you leave tonight. If you slump down and your knees hit that floor, then the next time I won't use the cutter whip on you, I will use the paddle. We both know that the paddle does nothing for you, don't we? So, will you be standing when I return?"

"Yes, Miss Trix" he replied while trying to steady himself.

I walked out the door and closed it behind me, then looked at my watch to make sure I had enough time.

The office that I used was down a level, so I quickly made my way towards the stairs. As I opened the door and pulled out the study books from my bag, I checked my watch again. Finding study time while working here five nights a week was hard. I often found myself trying not to fall asleep on the table late at night. Having a customer tied up for longer than I should was definitely not good for business.

"Trix, don't you have a customer?" I heard Max say as he came into the room and closed the door behind him.

"Yes, I do, I have given him ten minutes on the play rack".

"Okay, just make sure you keep your eye on your watch Trix" Max replied with humour in his tone.

"I will" I replied. "Actually, Max I have to talk to you about this weekend. I won't be able to work as my parents are coming home and have insisted that I see them over this time. I'm really sorry for the short notice".

"Trix, you are scheduled on for Friday night and you also have some regular customers booked. I can't see a way we can get around this. Any chance of you slipping out for a couple of hours at least? I know we have a birthday party of five coming in that night and I could really do with your help. I will make it worth your while" he replied.

I'd never had a birthday party client before and for some reason that excited me.

"I will have to see Max as I don't know when they are flying in. I will find out and let you know tomorrow, okay?".

Max looked at me, then walked over and pored himself a drink.

"Alright Trix, you can let me know. You had better make your way upstairs soon as your ten minutes is up".

I looked at my watch and he was correct.

Packing up my books slowly I caught a glimpse of Max out of the corner of my eye.

"What?" I said as I smiled back at him. "It doesn't hurt for them to wait a little longer you know".

Max laughed, then sat down behind the desk.

"I love your attitude Trix. Thank you for choosing to work at Elite" he said with that sly sexy grin he always used around us girls.

"You're welcome" I replied, as I opened and exited through the door.

Chapter 5

My parents arrived home Thursday afternoon, so I had to go straight there after university instead of to Elite. Luckily Max was understanding of my situation, and I had managed to convince my parents that I had a party to attend to on Friday night which gave me the excuse to go and work at Elite later that evening.

My mother, Isabella, was sitting in the formal lounge when I arrived home, looking like she had had more plastic surgery while they were away. Her face looked tight, and her bleach blonde hair was at the point of being so white that it made her teeth look slightly grey.

"Sarah, you're home. Let me have a look at you" she said as I walked towards her and was then enveloped in her Gucci perfume-filled hug.

"I really don't know how I had such a bright and intelligent daughter" she said.

She took a length of my hair in her hand and then dropped it quickly like it was some kind of deadly disease.

"How about this weekend we go and get your hair colour changed. It really is verging on bland brown now and a bit of colour will make your eyes pop. We could also see about getting just a slight amount of Botox to make sure you never get wrinkles. You're going to be twenty one in only a few weeks and there is no better time than the present to start preserving your lovely face" she said.

I had nearly forgotten about my birthday which was in three weeks' time. As I looked at her botoxed face, oversized collagen filled lips and bleached hair, I wondered where the mother that I had known as a child had gone to.

"I like my hair mum and I really don't agree in the whole Botox thing".

She recoiled slightly and looked as if I had just told her I was giraffe.

"You know, sometimes Sarah I do wonder if you were swapped at birth with another baby. Then I look at your father and realise that you look like him, just in a more feminine way".

There you have it, the insult I had been waiting for. Life never changed with my mother's underlying insults.

"Roger" my mother shouted. "Sarah is here, come and join us".

I heard the door click open to my father's office and the noise of his shoes echoed on the marble floor.

"Sarah, there you are. It's so good to see you again. How long has it been?"

"Three months, Dad" I replied. Not really long enough, I thought.

"Well let's open some champagne, we have something to celebrate".

He popped the bottle open and poured three glasses, handed my mother and I one each, then they both sat down opposite me.

"Sarah" my father started. "As you know, your mother and I are hardly home here in LA, and we have been spending our time between Italy, Germany and France. Well, your mother and I have purchased a home in Italy and have decided to make that our main base" he stopped, and I saw him look at my mother, who placed her hand on his, then nodded in reassurance.

"Go on" I said, waiting for the punch line.

"Well, your birthday is coming up soon and we thought that you would like to have something of your own rather than living in this large house with the staff".

"Well yes, it would be nice not to have to answer to Winston on my whereabouts" I replied.

"Precisely!" my father said.

"You see Sarah" my mother started "Your father and I would like to sell this house and Winston, plus the staff, will be moving to Italy to look after our new house. Now we know you're doing so well at university, so we don't want you to move away from your friends or your school. What we would like to do is to buy you your own apartment, in LA, where you will have a very substantial monthly allowance and can come and go as you please".

They both sat looking at me and I could see that they expected me to be upset by this news, but it was the opposite.

"That sounds amazing! I would love to have my own apartment in LA. Thank you!" I said, my enthusiasm a little too noticeable.

The relief on their faces was instant and my mother drank her drink quickly then walked over and hugged me awkwardly.

"Let's go shopping on Saturday. We have the real estate agent already notified and he has some fantastic properties to view. I'm so excited for you Sarah, and you can still come and visit us whenever you like" she said as she kissed me on the cheek and then walked towards the staircase to go up to her room.

"Sarah, this could be a whole new life for you, something new and exciting" my father said.

"Yes Dad, you're right. I couldn't be happier" I said and smiled.

Chapter 6

I could hear the commotion in the lounge bar all the way to the changing rooms. It seemed that the birthday party group had arrived.

"Looks like it's going to be a fun night girls!" Mandy, also known to her clients as Black Widow, said as she pulled on her latex glove.

Each dominatrix at Elite had their own distinct look. Mandy was in her forties but could easily pass for her thirties. She had the most curvaceous body out of all the dominatrix's that worked at Elite. Her backside was voluptuous and when she put on her latex dresses she looked like a black sexy Jessica Rabbit. Many of her regular clients hired her just so they could watch her, and her backside move around the room.

Daisy, aka Pure Fantasy, was the smallest dominatrix we had. She was an Asian girl whose character was based on the sexy, almost childlike, anime characters. The Japanese businessmen loved her.

Chantelle, known as Death Addiction, was the scariest looking out of all the girls. She had a part goth, part horror story, seductress look to her. Her clients were the rich fetish clients. Death Addiction was not afraid to give them exactly what they wanted, no matter how sick and twisted it seemed to all of us.

Tonight, I had decided to wear my favourite mid-calf length super tight latex black skirt and black latex top with cut outs exposing the sides and tops of my breasts. It actually gave the effect of being bound tightly by the latex and went lovely with my black lace up stiletto heels and red leather mistress mask which covered the area around my eyes. It was the type you would wear to an expensive mascaraed ball.

There was a knock at the door and Max opened it a second later.

"Girls you are all looking extremely sexy. We have some very unruly early twenties downstairs, and I want you to show them just how we deal with naughty boys. Show them some thrills but try not to make any spills".

We all laughed because it was on ongoing joke at Elite. If your client was not able to contain their excitement and made a mess, then you were buying a round of drinks after work.

"Trix, can I see you for a minute" Max said.

"Sure Max, just let me finish applying my mascara and I will be with you in a sec".

"Great, meet me in the viewing room just off the lounge, okay?".

I nodded and went back to applying the mascara quickly as he left the room.

"You know Trix, I have never seen Max have such a 'thing' for anyone like he does for you" Mandy said.

I was a bit taken back by the comment. Max was my boss, and I would never go there.

"You sound jealous Mandy" Chantelle said while applying her lipstick. "From what I heard you had a slice of Maxie-pie last Christmas at our get together".

Mandy looked at Chantelle and gave her the "whatever" look.

Everyone was waiting for Mandy to reply, but instead she just turned around and worked on her makeup.

I got up, pulled my skirt down over my hips, then walked down to the viewing room.

I knocked, entered and saw Max sitting on a stool in the bar area. This room had a special one-way mirror overlooking the lounge so we could see the clients without them seeing us. It reminded me of old police movies where they interrogated the villain while others watched secretly behind the mirrored wall.

"You look stunning tonight Trix, very 1930s inspired" Max said as his eyes wandered over my body.

"How old are you, Max?"

I didn't mean for it to come out like that, but I just seemed to blurt out what I was thinking.

Max laughed. " I turn 29 when we're away at the retreat Trix. Why do you ask?" he said.

"Sorry, I didn't mean to pry. I just wondered" I said, blushing slightly.

Max got off the stool and came towards me. He placed his hand on my shoulder then moved it down to my arm to my fingers. His touch sent shivers down my spine, and I couldn't help but feel the heat rising around my neck and face.

"You know, you look truly beautiful when you blush, Mistress Trix" he whispered.

He looked at me with his green eyes and I couldn't help but look back at him. For some reason he made me nervous, but also very curious. I did find him attractive and very sexy, but he was my boss, and I knew I couldn't go there.

Max seemed to sense this and released my hand, then we both moved over towards the glass.

" I brought you here not to seduce you Trix, but to show you the birthday boy. He will be your client tonight and he has also requested something slightly different. I don't know whether you will want to do this request, as it's not something you have done with any client before".

A feeling of dread started to fill me because although I loved being a dominatrix, I wasn't into fulfilling some of the clients desires like Death Addiction did.

I looked into the room and saw a group of early-to-mid-twenty year old males drinking at the bar. At first, I thought I was seeing things and then I looked again and gasped. Max looked at me concerned.

"What is it?"

"I know them, they go to my university. I can't do this Max, what if they recognise me?".

Max looked at the group and then at me.

"I think I can handle this".

He pulled his phone out from his jacket and then I heard the phone dial ringing and a woman's voice answer.

"Stephanie, this is Max from Elite. I need your help, it's urgent. Can you arrange to send over the full cat suit with attached head covering. Yes, that one. I will pay you whatever you want but I need it here in half an hour at the latest. Come to the back door and I will meet you. Fantastic, you're amazing".

With that he hung up the phone and turned to me.

"Go and redo your makeup. I need you to blacken your eye makeup more and grab the jade green contact lenses. Get one of the girls to show you how to put them in. The suit I have ordered is a full catsuit with a fully covered head cat mask and tail. Tonight, you're going to be every man's fantasy girl, cat woman".

I smiled and was just about to leave the room to get ready when I turned back towards the window.

"Which one is the birthday boy client that I'm looking after and what is the special request?".

Max looked at them standing by the bar and pointed his finger towards the end of the bar.

"White dress top, black pants, looks nervous. The request is that you kiss him after each punishment and not a peck on the lips. This boy has requested it 'with passion'.

I looked to where Max was pointing and felt slightly dizzy. Standing there leaning against the bar with his friends was Mitch Bradley.

I wet my dry lips and felt the butterflies in my stomach start to flutter. I would have to be careful to disguise my voice a little. Hopefully this cat suit had enough to cover my face and prevent him from recognising me.

Max was waiting for my answer and looked a little concerned at the time I was taking.

"I would be happy to make his birthday special" I said.

"Good girl. Go get ready and I will drop the catsuit into you soon. I had better go and get the girls to start on some of these boys before they drink my bar dry".

As I walked towards the changing room, I couldn't help but feel nervous. Mitch was my crush at school and had been for years. I would need to be careful about how I handled this as I couldn't give myself away.

Starting on the contouring of my eyes with black makeup and then applying bright red kiss proof lipstick, I suddenly found myself getting excited. It wasn't because I was able to give him a fantastic birthday dominatrix experience, but because I now had permission to kiss the guy I had fantasized about for years, and I could do it with the passion I had always dreamt about. I also loved the fact that he wouldn't know that it was plain, brainy, strait-laced Sarah underneath the latex.

Tonight, I was going to give him the best Mistress Trix experience he could ever ask for, and I was going to love every minute of it.

Chapter 7

The catsuit fit my body like a glove. It showed every curve and accentuated my breasts with a peep hole feature showing off the top of my cleavage.

A sewn-in tail climbed up the back, where the catsuit zipped, and curved around the top of my buttock area. The legs of the catsuit had small cut openings, allowing you to see little areas of skin showing through, which I found very erotic. The mask was a full mask that I pulled over my head and it had enough room for my ponytail to come through the back and for my eyes and mouth to be shown. Everything else was covered in black latex.

I put on the latex black gloves and tight leather stiletto boots and when I looked in the mirror, I couldn't help feeling aroused by the vision staring back.

Max knocked and then opened the door. I looked at him as his eyes wandered over my body. I felt extremely powerful at that moment and Max knew it.

"You know, if I had known that you would look this amazing then I would have given you this as a special treat for your birthday and not just for some guys first time at Elite. You're a complete knock out Trix, and I'm in awe of just how confident, sexy and utterly beautiful you look".

I could tell he was turned on by this new version of me and I had to say that if I didn't have Mitch Bradley waiting for me, then I probably would have thanked Max with a kiss. I felt beautiful and empowered standing in front of him and it wasn't like the thought hadn't crossed my mind before, but we all knew the number one rule here was hands off the Management.

I walked up to him and smiled.

"Thanks Max, maybe we should get this show started".

He moved aside and opened the door for me as I walked out and continued down the corridor into my room.

Locking the door behind me I looked to the side and could see Mitch sitting on the couch waiting. He stood up as soon as he saw me, and I could tell he was nervous.

"Hi. Listen, I have never done this before so I'm a little nervous. I have been told that you know what I would like and that you have agreed to it, so thank you".

I walked slowly over to him, making sure he saw every movement of my body accentuated in the latex.

"I have been told about your desires and I will make sure they are fulfilled. What you don't know though is that I'm in control here, in this room, and from now on you will only answer when I ask you a question and you will do everything that I ask you to do without question. You will say 'Yes Mistress Trix' and you will not scream out unless I tell you to. You will not place one hand on my body unless I ask you to, and I will tell you where you can place that hand. Our code word here is Tricky, and you must use this if you want me to stop. But understand this, once you have used this word then the fun stops and you leave. Your time with me is for half an hour and when it's finished you will have a shower in the adjoining bathroom, dress and leave. Do you understand the terms of this contract?".

I watched him swallow hard and then nod in agreement.

"Good. Now take off your clothes and place them on the hangers in the bathroom. You can choose to do this naked or be in your briefs, I will leave that up to you. You have exactly thirty seconds to undress and be back here in front of me".

I made my way over to the wall compartments that hid my whips and chains to bind him in.

When I turned around, he was standing in his fitted boxer briefs which was a slight disappointment as I was hoping to see every part of Mitch Bradley.

His body was chiselled, and he had abs that stopped just before his Hugo Boss trunks. His arms were muscular and as I recalled him in his school shirt, they were always my favourite part on his body. Well, they were certainly up there in the top two.

"Stand with your feet facing the wall, hip width apart and place your arms out to your sides" I instructed.

He moved over and did as he was told. I fastened the leather straps around his wrists and ankles and then attached the chains to them. The chains were attached to the sides of the wall, then to a pulley system that allowed me to stretch them tight. I pressed a button and the chains retracted within the wall cavity.

I moved towards him, so I was standing with my breasts pushed against his back. I pulled his head back to the side and then kissed him passionately. He responded straight away and the chemistry between us ignited.

I pulled back and whispered in his ear "that is just a small taste of more to come".

I felt him shiver slightly and noticed he was already breathing deeper.

Taking my soft leather whip in my hand I pulled back to half of what I would normally give my clients and hit him over the buttocks. He didn't whimper but made a guttural sound of pleasure.

I pulled the whip back further and hit him again, this time over his back. It wasn't strong enough to leave a mark, but I could see that he was enjoying it.

"Would you like it harder, birthday boy?" I said making sure my voice was assertive and nothing like my Sarah voice.

"Yes, Mistress Trix".

I pulled the whip back and hit him again, this time hard enough to leave red marks over his back.

His whole body spasmed and I could see his knees shaking slightly.

I moved against his back again, pulled his head towards me and kissed him passionately once more.

The kiss lasted longer this time as our tongues moved seamlessly against each other. I pulled back and went over to my drawer, where I grabbed the paddle and a large peacock feather.

I placed the peacock feather in my left hand and the paddle in my right. Stroking the peacock feather up his legs and over his buttocks and groin area I heard him moan softly. I took the paddle and hit him hard on his right buttock. The shock was almost instant, and he cried out.

"Did I say you could cry out, birthday boy? I don't think so!"

I brought back the paddle and hit him on his left buttock. He moved but the sound of his delight was kept to a minimum through his clenched teeth.

I moved the peacock feather over his buttocks and around to the front of his body, making sure I moved it over his now fully aroused member and up to his chest. The look on his face was so beautiful, as I don't think I've ever seen what pleasure was to him before now.

I moved to his back again and struck him over his buttock with the paddle. His knees buckled and he collapsed down on the floor.

Unchaining him, I helped him up and then moved him over to the soft padded leather table. This table always reminded me of the beds they used in asylums for mental patients as it had cuffs on the feet and hands plus a belt that went around the middle. The only difference is this one was made out of bright red leather and was used to afflict pleasure not pain.

I strapped him down to the bed, so he was unable to move and then climbed on top of him, straddling him.

I bent down and kissed him passionately until I knew that kissing him any further would mean I would be buying drinks for the girls at the end of the night.

He looked up at me as I straddled him and I could see in his eyes that he wanted more, that he wanted to touch me.

I looked up to where the camera was based, as I knew Max would be watching this and untied his left hand from the restraints and brought his hand up to my mouth. I took his middle finger in my mouth and sucked it from the tip to the knuckle as his eyes rolled slightly back, like he was trying to concentrate on not exploding. I then placed his hand on my latex covered breast and squeezed his hand around it.

"Happy birthday" I purred.

Placing his hand back in the restraint I climbed off him and went and retrieved the one thing that I knew would give him the finale to his birthday.

As I walked towards him, I couldn't help feeling a little sad that our half hour was over. I had fun and had done things I had never done with any of my clients. As far as touching me, it was never allowed, and sucking his finger was something that I never did with any client and had never wanted to. But I wanted to go as far as I could with Mitch and push the boundaries as far as I was allowed to without getting into trouble.

Showing Mitch what was I my hand, I clamped his nipples gently, stood back and then pressed the button in my hand. He cried out and then quickly shut his mouth to keep the sound in. His body writhed under the pleasure of it, and I knew he was close now. I pressed the button again and his body calmed down, but he was panting heavily.

I didn't want to see him climax in this way, call me selfish but I wanted to see that as Sarah and not as Mistress Trix.

He was breathing heavily as I removed the nipple clamps. I moved my hands over his chest as he moaned and then I kissed him one last time, this time longer and deeper.

I untied him from the table and then pointed to the bathroom door.

"Your time with me is over. You can take a shower and get dressed then use the door beside the shower, it will take you back to your friends waiting in the lounge".

"Thank you, Mistress Trix. It was the most amazing experience I've ever had".

I smiled briefly and then walked towards the door.

"Yes, I'm sure it was".

Chapter 8

Max had been avoiding me for the last two weeks.

I didn't know what his issue was, and he wasn't telling me either. I had tried to talk to him about it, but he always replied with "it's nothing, Trix".

I knew that he had obviously witnessed what I did with Mitch and that it was different than what I would normally do with my clients, but I did it because I was caught up in the moment and I wanted to show Mitch what he was missing.

At university, I had walked past Mitch several times during the past two weeks and each time he was busy talking to his friends and never seemed to notice me. How powerless I felt as Sarah! Every day I wanted to finish school and rush over to Elite where I could take off my restrictive clothing and become Trix.

Chris and Jayden ran up to me at lunch and grabbed me by the hand. They led me outside to the benches that we always sat at, which were unoccupied and further away from everyone else.

My stomach started to do flips and I was nervous about what they were going to say. I had hoped that Mitch hadn't guessed who I was, and my disguise was good enough so that it wouldn't give me away. There was still that seed of doubt that one day I would walk into class and all eyes would be turned to me and my secret would be out.

"Girl, you are going to scream when you hear this" Jayden said, full of enthusiasm.

Chris looked at me and raised his eyebrows as if to say, 'just you wait'.

I sat down with them, and Jayden leaned forward.

"Did you hear that it was a certain person's birthday a couple of weekends ago and on that night this certain person stopped by Elite with his boy-crew to see some dominatrix's?"

Oh god, I felt slightly sick.

I put my best surprised face on while feeling the heat rising around my neck.

"Go on" I said.

"Well, this certain person is also the same person you have had a crush on like forever, a certain Mitch Bradley".

Jayden stopped and I made sure to look totally shocked and even a little horrified.

"Who told you this?" I whispered.

Chris looked at me and whispered.

"Well, I overheard two of Mitch's friends talking about it in the changing rooms this morning. Turns out that Mitch said it was the most amazing experience he has ever had and that he had to try and stop himself from exploding while the woman was straddling him and sucking on his finger".

Jayden and Chris both looked at each other and laughed together.

I was nervous about what to say next, so I just said, "Oh that's weird".

"Darling, I think the only thing that is weird is that the boy was nearly going to blow his load over a sucked finger. Imagine what a disappointment he would be when someone does the real thing on him".

Chris laughed out loud at Jayden's explanation, I blushed and then gave a short kind of half laugh.

"Does anyone else know about this?" I said.

Jayden looked at Chris and then smiled, "only half the university".

That was typical of these boys, they could never keep anything to themselves.

The rest of the day went by in a bit of a blur, but I could see the gossipers chatting away and then moving the story along like it was wildfire.

By the end of the day Mitch looked very red in the face as everyone was making some comment or patting him on the back.

I caught his eye as I walked down the hallway and for a brief second, he looked at me and smiled, then quickly went back to his friends.

There is no way that I was ever going to get a chance with Mitch Bradley while I was plain Sarah. Luckily, I had Mistress Trix's memories of that night to keep alive.

The moving date was set for next week as the apartment my parents had brought for me had now been settled through the lawyers. We had all decided on a stunning two-bedroom Oceanfront Penthouse Apartment, which I fell in love with immediately. The views were amazing, and the terrace overlooked the clear blue ocean. I already had the painters changing the interior colours to white and the furniture I had picked out was in deep greys, silvers, burnt orange and teal blues. I wanted to have that beach feel to it so it would match the coastline and sunsets.

My parents stayed around only for that weekend, signed the papers and handed me an unlimited credit card to do any changes I wanted and buy furniture. I hugged them goodbye before they flew back to Italy, knowing that I would probably see them next at Christmas, and only briefly at that.

I know it sounds terrible, but I felt more at home with my friends at university and the people at Elite than I did with my own parents. Although I knew that they loved me, I always felt more like a hand me down bag rather than their daughter.

Moving into my own place was going to be amazing because I had no one to answer to and could make the space completely my own. I had also decided not to use the card unless it was for emergencies. I was earning fantastic money now and really didn't need to rely on my parents for the expenses. I told my parents that I had a part time job working at a lawyer's firm in town and that I didn't need the card, but they insisted on me having it and using it whenever I wanted.

Friday rolled around fast enough, and I was getting ready in the changing room when Max's secretary Kitty opened the door in a panic.

"Trix, you have an unannounced appointment waiting for you in the lounge".

"What? Didn't they make an appointment with us?"

"No, he just turned up with some others, so we thought he was a regular. Turns out he isn't but has been here before".

Panic started to kick in as I wondered if it could be Mitch.

I followed Kitty down to the viewing room and sitting in the lounge was Mitch dressed in a business suit. He looked very handsome.

"Where is Max?" I said suddenly very nervous.

"He's taken the night off. He said he needed some time away so left me in charge" Kitty replied.

That's typical! Just when I needed Max he's taking a personal day off, I thought.

Luckily, after the urgent need of the cat woman costume, I had decided to invest in some more full body, head covering outfits.

"Kitty, stall him with another drink, then bring him into the room in about 20 minutes. I need to change and do my makeup differently. I will also need the jade-coloured contacts again".

She disappeared out the door and I turned back to the glass. He didn't look as nervous as his first time here, which could mean trouble for me.

I opened the door to leave just as Kitty walked into the lounge and offered him a drink.

Back in the dressing room I picked out the pieces I thought would be best this time. I chose my fishnet black stockings, tight one-piece bondage swimsuit in latex, red and black push up corset to go over the top, thigh high stiletto heels and the bondage mask with my false blonde ponytail pulled out the back of the mask, with only my eyes and mouth shown. There was something quite seductive about wearing a mask and only revealing my eyes and mouth. It felt mysterious.

When I opened the door to the room Mitch was sitting on the same couch wearing black tight boxers, which showed of his masculinity nicely.

"Hello birthday boy, it's nice to see you again. I see that you have decided to come back for another session. What can I offer you tonight?"

"Hello Mistress Trix. I would like you to show me more tonight and I would also like to have the same terms that we had last time".

I looked at him standing there and wondered how far I could take it with him. Obviously, he liked what he had last time so maybe some harder whips and this time I would also use something new on him to make it extra special.

"Alright Birthday boy, go and stand with your feet facing the wall and we shall begin".

"Yes, Mistress Trix" he replied and walked over to the wall then spread his legs apart and opened his arms out to each side.

I whipped him harder this time and left him with red welt marks on his back. He became so aroused that I wondered if he was going to finish straight away.

I let him down off the rack and then turned him around with his back against the wall. I pinned his hands to the wall and then kissed him fully slipping my tongue deep into his mouth. I knew he wanted to touch me but tonight I wasn't going to allow it. I would kiss him with all the passion I could give but the power was still mine and I wasn't going to give him that tonight.

While he was still standing against the wall I went to my drawer and pulled out the device I thought he might like to try.

I placed some moisturiser on my latex glove and then walked over to him. He saw the leather straps in my hands, but I could see that he obviously didn't know what it was.

"Now Birthday boy, I am going to show you this item and you can decide if you want to use it, or not. Do you know what this is?"

I held my hand out so he could see it and he shook his head.

"This is a cock harness with a special cock ring attached. It slows the blood flow so that you don't make a mess on my floor. It will also make you harder for longer. Would you like to try this?"

I could see the excitement in his eyes as he whispered "Yes, Mistress Trix. Yes, please".

"Remove your underwear".

He did as I instructed, and I couldn't help but look at his manhood. It was larger than most of my clients and he had obviously shaven recently as the area was very smooth.

"Now look at my eyes only. Don't look at my hands".

He stayed looking at my eyes as I slipped my hand down with the ring between my fingers and moved it down onto his hard shaft.

I could feel him tremble and knew that he was seconds away from climaxing.

"Now take a deep breath and calm your breathing. You don't want the fun to end, do you?

He took a deep breath in and then replied "No, Mistress Trix".

I brought him forward a couple of steps and then fastened the straps around his buttocks.

"You will have to take this off in the shower after because you will have a reaction straight away when you take it off. Do you understand?".

"Yes, Mistress Trix, I understand".

"Good, now I will place something between your mouth first because you are going to scream out and this will allow you to bite down on something. I'm also going to blindfold you and tie your hands behind your back".

I pulled out a ball gag from the drawer and the soft leather flogger. I placed the ball gag in his mouth and tied it to the back of his head. I grabbed the blindfold and felt the silk slip gently between my hands then placed it over his eyes and tied his hands behind his back.

I stood back and slowly draped the flogger over his member. I watched as it became even more erect and his body spasmed and shivered in delight.

Taking the flogger in my hand, I hit him a little harder and he bit down on the ball and moaned. I hit him again and this time harder. I saw his muscles clench in his arms as he bent over and when he stood back up, I could see that his member had become engorged which meant he was about to erupt.

"Now listen carefully to me Birthday Boy. You are just on the edge now and pretty soon you are going to dirty my floor, so I'm going to release your hands and pull the gag out from your mouth. I'm going to kiss you one last time and then flog you one last time. You're going to remove the blindfold and head straight to the bathroom".

I moved behind him and released his hands.

I felt him quiver as I took out the gag and kissed him plunging my tongue into his mouth. I pulled back my hand and brought the flogger down on him. He bent over, removed the blindfold and ran into the bathroom.

I heard him cry out in ecstasy in the bathroom as I walked out the door, smiling.

Chapter 9

Summer break was here and so was my birthday. I invited over the usual crowd from university for a private drinking session and had taken off the following day from work so I could enjoy the beach and get a tan.

Flowers had arrived in the morning along with a large box. I recognised the box straight away and knew that it had to be from Max. I opened it quickly and inside was a red and black leather flogger, red handcuffs and a dress made from beautiful black leather. It was so soft to touch that I had to try it on immediately.

The fit was perfect, and it clung to my body in all the right ways. The cleavage was quite revealing, which I loved, and the dress was full length and split up each side, exposing my legs right up to the thigh. The shoes were next to the dress in the box and as I lifted them out, I thought they were a work of art. They were black with silver studs on them, and the wedge heel was cut away so that it looked like you were practically holding yourself up by air.

I looked for a card within the flowers and when I opened it the message read:

'Very beautiful xx M'.

Looking at myself in the mirror I had to agree.

I couldn't wear the outfit with my friends coming over, so I quickly put it back in the box and placed it gently in the closet. I would take it to the Retreat next week when I was away with Max and the rest of the girls who worked at Elite.

Jayden, Chris, Tori, Dale and a few other friends from school turned up around six and we sat out on the large balcony overlooking the ocean drinking cocktails and champagne. My parents had sent me an early birthday present last week in the form of a brand-new black BMW convertible and two cases of French champagne. The gifts were amazing, but I still wished that I could have seen them for my birthday and would happily give the gifts back for that. Unfortunately, they were heading to Monte Carlo again as my father had some work there and I presumed my mother had more plastic surgery planned.

The topic soon turned to the gossip that had been going around university for the last month of Mitch and his friends going to Elite. I was now used to hearing this conversation and it really didn't worry me anymore. In fact, I wondered if Mitch had said anything about his return to Elite and our second session.

"You know he lives on this same stretch of this beach, don't you?" Jayden said.

"What? No, I didn't know that" I stammered, nearly chocking on my drink.

"Yes, he lives about four houses down actually. His parents are a bit like yours Sarah, always away overseas" Chris said.

"Well, I haven't seen him around here, but then again I have been quite busy working" I suddenly stopped and then tried to regain my composure.

"Yes, how is it going working for a boring law firm? In fact, I'm really not sure why you work because you parents have given you an unlimited credit card that you can use whenever you like. If it was me then I would be out shopping all day" Dale said, drinking the last of her cocktail.

"I work because I don't want them to pay for everything, plus I love what I do". That wasn't a lie, it was absolutely the truth.

"Well, if you ask me, I think we should get drunk, go down to the beach and light a bonfire and roast marshmallows" Tori said.

We all raised our glasses up and clinked them together.

"Here's to Sarah's birthday. May she get shitfaced tonight and finally get laid by the man of her dreams" Chris shouted.

I couldn't agree more!

The party was in full swing, and more friends had turned up to the bonfire. Drinks were being passed around along with the s'mores.

I was feeling very drunk and noticed my words slurring slightly. I stood up to head into the house to fetch another bottle when I tripped over someone who was standing not far from me. As I landed on the soft sand, I heard Chris and Jayden laughing behind me "Sarah's shitfaced, better call it a night".

I lay there for a second and then felt hands come around my back and under my arms. I was suddenly lifted into a standing position.

"You okay, Sarah?" I heard.

When I looked at who had helped me, I had to stop myself and wonder if I was really that drunk.

It was Mitch.

"Oh yeah, sure I'm okay, just a little drunk" I slurred.

"I can see that. Do you want some help getting to your apartment? Your party seems to be dying down now anyway, so I can help you clear up if you like".

I stared at him and kept blinking as I was seeing two of him in front of me.

"You called me Sarah" I slurred.

"Yes, well that is your name, isn't it? Unless you have another name, you want me to call you?"

I looked at him wondering if he knew, but my drunk brain soon realised the comment was more meant to be a joke then him knowing I was Mistress Trix.

"No other name, just plain Sarah" I laughed.

"Well, I wouldn't go that far Sarah. You're certainly not plain" he said.

I looked into his eyes then felt the room spinning slightly and knew I was going to throw up.

"Um, can you excuse me" I said as I raced towards the bathroom joined to the outdoor pool area.

I was pretty sure that this was turning out to be the worst night of my life as I threw up all the contents of the drinks and s'mores. When I had finally stopped throwing up, I came out and Mitch was gone.

Making my way up to the apartment I berated myself for being such an idiot, but how was I to know that he was going to be there?

Locking the front door behind me, I sank into my comfortable bed and turned out the light and tried to not think of how embarrassing that was.

Oh well, there goes any hope of ever being with him!

Chapter 10

I woke up with my head hammering and some vague memory of seeing Mitch at the bonfire last night.

Getting out of bed, I surveyed the damage of the party. Luckily the party had been positioned down on the beach and as I looked over the balcony, I could see that there was only a faint circle where the bonfire had been and everything else had been cleared away already.

Mental note to-self, give the cleaners a tip!

I looked around the room and although it didn't look too bad, I was so house proud now that I couldn't see anything but empty bottles, big jugs of cocktail mixes, leftover pizza and mess that needed cleaning.

Deciding to take a shower first, I heard a knock at the door, so quickly rinsed off my hair and wrapped a towel around me.

Thinking it was probably Jayden or Chris coming back to get something they forgot, I opened the door only to see Mitch standing there.

I yelped slightly, then slammed the door in his face.

"Sorry, just a minute, I have to get dressed".

"No worries" he said, laughing.

After putting on my bikini and my jean shorts with a top over them, I quickly applied some mascara and a bit of lip gloss. Looking in the mirror I still looked a bit pale, but it would have to do.

I opened the door to see Mitch leaning against the railing, in board shorts and a t-shirt.

"Sorry, I'm not really used to visitors" I laughed.

"Me neither, actually. I just came by to see if you would like any help cleaning up".

I looked around the room and then back at Mitch.

"Um sure, would you like a coffee?".

"That would be great" he replied.

Mitch came in and we walked over to the kitchen where I put the coffee machine on.

"Nice place you have here, are you living alone?"

"Yes, my parents live in Italy now, so we brought this place about a month ago. I love having my own place though, it's nice not to have to answer to anyone".

"I agree with that. My parents are never home and have another home in Switzerland where they stay for ten months of the year, so the beach house is mine really".

"So, we have the life that most kids our age would only ever dream of. Funny how you would give that all away just to have a relationship with your parents".

He was silent for a bit and then nodded.

"Sorry, I didn't mean to imply that you were like that".

He looked at me for what seemed like the longest time, then smiled.

"You're actually correct and it's weird that you see it exactly as I do" he said.

I smiled, then poured the coffee.

"So, I hear you work for a law office in town as well as going to university. That must be interesting" he said.

"Yeah, I really enjoy it" I said quickly. "What about you? What do you get up to in your spare time?"

As soon as I said the words, I regretted it. Now he is going to think I was asking him about Elite.

"Well, if you listen to rumours then you know that I like to see a dominatrix in my spare time" he smiled awkwardly.

I breathed in slightly while I gathered my thoughts as to what to say next.

"So, it's true then?"

"Yes, it's true. I went to a private club called Elite and saw a dominatrix called Mistress Trix".

"Okay, so what was it like?" I asked.

"It was mind blowing actually. I have never felt so aroused by anyone in my life. It was like I found someone that I can experiment with and enjoy being with them in a totally different way. It was so sexy".

I blushed and looked at my coffee as I didn't want him to see my elation that he liked what I did.

"Sorry, I should probably have kept that to myself, I've not talked to anyone about that part. I told my friends one story but kept that to myself".

Smiling briefly, I was glad that he was telling me this and that I was Sarah, not Mistress Trix.

"It's okay. I'm glad you told me. Have you been back again?"

"Yes, I went back a couple of weeks ago and have had to stop myself from going back again. I feel a kind of addiction to Mistress Trix and the fact that I can't touch her when I want to so badly, well it drives me crazy".

"What about your other relationships, surely you would be able to experience these things with someone else in a real relationship?".

"Unfortunately, no, well not really. I have had a few women, but I can't seem to climax with them like I do around her. I don't know if it is the dominatrix side or just how she makes me feel, but I really want to be with her in every way possible".

I couldn't help contain my elation and if I was dressed as Mistress Trix now I would have ripped his clothes off here in the kitchen and made sure he knew just how I really felt about him.

"Well maybe you shouldn't stay away, you never know, underneath every latex outfit could be a woman you could fall in love with".

He smiled and looked at my eyes. "Thanks Sarah, I might just do that. Now let's get on to the cleaning of this place as it might take us a while" he laughed.

What a miracle Mitch's words had on me because the hangover soon went, and we worked together till the afternoon when he had to leave.

As I waved goodbye, I couldn't wait to get back to Elite to see whether he had made an appointment.

———◉———

THE WEEK PASSED BY, and Mitch didn't return to Elite. He wasn't away as I saw him most days when he would either come over to my place or I would go to his. I made up the excuse that I was going away to see my parents for the following week when I was going on the retreat.

I couldn't understand why he hadn't come back yet. Maybe he had decided that Mistress Trix would never be interested in him that way. If only he knew that it would be the opposite.

With my bags packed, he waved goodbye and walked back along the beach while I caught a taxi out to the airport. We planned to have dinner together at my place when I returned, so at least Sarah was able to spend time with him

Mistress Trix would have to wait.

Chapter 11

Arriving at the retreat, I couldn't believe how beautiful it was. Each girl had their own chalet, secured by gates and Max had given us our own personal access code. The chalet had two main living areas, plus a bedroom, bathroom and outside area where I had my own private swimming and jacuzzi. One of the bedrooms was stocked with what looked like the same equipment that we had at Elite and strangely, it looked like it had been there all the time, like this room was made specifically for that.

The bedroom was gorgeous and designed with my favourite colours, blues, silvers, burnt orange and white, the same colours that I had at my beach house.

As I unpacked my suitcase and hung my dominatrix outfits up in the master bedroom, I heard the gate open, which was a surprise as I thought no one could open it apart from me.

I looked outside to see Max walking up the pathway. He was dressed in his dark blue business suit with a white shirt that was open by one button at the top. He looked incredibly handsome.

"Hey Trix, how do you like it?" He said gesturing his arms out wide to show he meant the retreat.

"It's beautiful Max, thank you so much for making me come here. It's actually nice to have a different change of scenery. You get so used to the room at Elite that it sometimes just becomes a little mundane".

He smiled, then nodded and walked inside. I noticed that he kept looking at me when he thought I couldn't see him doing it, which was a little unusual.

We sat down on the couch by the open doors that led out to the patio, and I could see that he looked happier, which was a change from recently. He had been very distant at work lately and I wondered if there was something else going on in his life.

"Listen Trix, we have a few clients booked in tomorrow for you and about three each day for half-hour sessions over this next week. You also have Friday and Saturday off at the end of the week, as does everyone else. The trip here is about work but I also feel that we all need a little bit of downtime, so treat it like a mini holiday, okay?".

"Sounds great" I said watching him closely as he kept gripping his fingers together and looked nervous.

"Max is everything okay?"

He cleared his throat and licked his lips.

"Trix, as you may have noticed, I've been a bit distant ever since the birthday boy and his crew turned up at Elite and I felt that I needed some time to just work out what was going on. I have worked at Elite for the past five years and women have come and gone in that time, and I've been very vigilant to never form an attachment or feelings towards them".

He stopped and took a deep breath, then continued.

"When I saw the video of you with him and you letting him touch you, well I was completely jealous. You see Trix, I have never had a relationship with any of the girls at Elite and only once did I break my rule of sleeping with someone, which was a massive mistake".

I could see a small amount of perspiration start on his brow and I watched him as he quickly brushed his fingers through his hair.

"What I want to tell you, and you don't need to respond today as I just want you to think about it, is that I'm very attracted to the beautiful, confident woman that you are and I'm falling for you Trix. I want us to be together, in a relationship".

I nearly fell off my chair and had to close my mouth quickly. It was a lot to take in.

I knew I was very attracted to Max and when I'm near him I feel an amazing amount of chemistry between us, but was that enough? Did we know each other enough to begin any type of relationship, and what about my work at Elite?

I thought about Mitch, who I hadn't seen at Elite for nearly a month and for all I knew had decided to stop coming. I looked at Max and knew that he was genuine in what he was saying.

"Max, I'm a little shocked actually. I never thought you would be sitting here telling me this, as I know you're very strict about work relationships. I am very attracted to you and the chemistry we have has been so transparent that a lot of the staff have commented on it. I'm not saying no, I'm not saying yes. I just need a little bit of time to think it over, okay?"

He nodded, then stood up.

"Trix, you can have as much time as you need. I'm not going to pressure you into anything and if it's a no then we will still work together, and I will get over it in time. I promise not to be distant towards you, like I have been lately. Do we have a deal?"

I smiled and then gave him my hand like we were going to shake on it. Instead, he took my hand and raised it to his lips and kissed it then pulled me in towards him.

His lips touched mine and it was like an electric shock coursing through my body. His tongue thrust deeply into my mouth, and I moaned aloud as it sent waves of sensations through my body. We moved back against the wall, and he kissed me with such passion that I could feel my knees getting weak and my heart was racing in my chest.

As he leaned into me, I could feel he was rock hard against my stomach, and I knew I wanted more.

Max pulled away and then kissed me again softly on the lips.

"I adore you Trix, but I won't take this further because I don't want it to be about what I want. If you want to be with me, as in a relationship not a one-night stand, then here is the number to my chalet. Call me and I will be here".

He kissed me again passionately before buttoning up his jacket and walking out the door.

When the door closed, I sank to the floor breathless.

That night I had the most erotic dreams about Max.

In my dreams I was part Trix and part Sarah. He was kissing me deeply and moving on top of me. Our naked bodies clung together, and I felt possessed by him. His body was warm and muscular and as he positioned himself above me, I could feel his hardness pressing against me, wanting me to open up to him.

"I love you Trix. I love you" he whispered in my ear, and I felt his hot breath tingling against my neck.

He moved himself back and I felt myself opening up to him.

"Now, please, now" I begged.

Just as I felt him move into me, I woke up.

I was panting and the bed was drenched with sweat. The dream had been so real, and I screamed aloud because it was over, and I couldn't go back to it.

Sitting up, I felt my heart racing and knew what I wanted to do.

I found the number on my bed stand and called it. It rang for a few seconds and then he answered it.

"Trix? Are you okay?" he said, concern in his voice.

"No, I'm not. Can you come here please?".

"I'm leaving now. Are you okay Trix?"

"Yes, please hurry".

The phone went dead, and I knew he would be here soon. I grabbed my robe and quickly took the sheets off the bed and threw them in the laundry hamper.

I was just replacing the sheet when I heard the gate open and Max running up the pathway.

His first banged on the door a second later and I opened it quickly.

It had obviously been raining, which I hadn't even realised, and his shirt and hair were now dripping wet.

"Trix are you okay? You sounded really out of breath on the phone. Has something happened?"

I nodded. "I had a dream and I needed you."

"Was it something bad, like a nightmare?"

"No" I replied.

"Then what was it about?"

I walked towards him and started unbuttoning his shirt.

"It was about us. I dreamt about us" I said.

He stopped my hands from unbuttoning the last button and held them down by his waist.

"Trix, are you telling me that your answer is, yes? That you are going to give us a go?"

I looked at him then stood on my toes and kissed him. "Yes"

His hands released mine and he picked me up so that my legs were wrapped around him.

Max walked over to the bed and placed me gently down then undid the last button of his shirt and threw it aside.

He took off the rest of his clothes quickly and lay down beside me and untied my robe. He looked at me with pure lust in his eyes and kissed me.

His kisses were feverish, and we explored each other with our tongues. His hands moved over my breasts, and he took my nipples between his fingers and flicked them softly sending waves of ecstasy through me. He moved his head down to my breasts and licked each nipple with the point of his tongue. I moaned allowed and arched my back up.

I felt him harden against me and as I moved my hand over him, he made a deep guttural moan.

"Oh Trix, please" he said as he grew harder within my hand.

I was becoming wet. I knew I couldn't contain myself much longer and needed him inside me.

"Max, I want you. I need you. Please Max, please" I begged.

He kissed me passionately as he positioned himself over me then with one swift movement, I opened myself up to him and he thrust his long, thick shaft, deep inside me.

Our bodies moved together in unison. The feeling was unlike anything I had ever experienced before, and I felt myself building to climax.

His thrusts became more powerful and sensual with each move. I placed my fingers around him and moved them up and down his shaft with each thrust.

"Trix you're driving me insane, but I don't want to stop. I want to stay here forever".

I smiled at him then moved him over, so he was lying on his back. I lowered myself down on to him and closed my eyes, moaning at the share pleasure of his thickness. Moving in a rhythm with him and seeing the pleasure on his face was so thrilling and I knew I was going to climax soon. I massaged my breasts with my hands and pinched my nipples between my fingers and felt the warmth of my climax start to lubricate him.

His back arched up as I raised myself up and slowly lowered all the way down onto him. Seeing that I was close to climaxing he moved me on to my back and kissed me deeper, then thrust powerfully into me.

I moaned out loud with each movement as I felt the two of us climaxing together. His hot, wet liquid spilled into me as I felt my own enveloping him.

Exhausted we lay in each other's arms kissing and gently caressing each other's bodies.

"Trix, you're the most amazing woman. I could stay inside you for ever".

"Unfortunately, that would look very strange, although I would also love that" I replied, as I kissed him gently on his chest.

"Can I make a request though" I said.

"Anything" he replied.

"When we're not working and we are like this, can you call me Sarah and not Trix".

He leant over and kissed me again.

"Of course, Sarah".

As he kissed me deeply, I could feel our bodies come alive as if we were connected to each other by an invisible force.

Making love every spare moment we could throughout the week and getting to know his romantic and caring side, meant that I forgot about the relationship that I had wanted so badly with Mitch and decided that the friendship we had now would remain just that. I was going to give my heart to Max and put myself into this relationship.

I was still going to work as Trix, as I still loved my job, even though Max offered for me to stop. I didn't see anything sexual with any of my clients and Max knew that, so I was happy to still become the woman I wanted to be when I was Mistress Trix.

At the end of the week, I flew out from the retreat happier than I had ever been and more sexually alive then I had ever felt. As I pulled up to the house, I saw Mitch waiting for me with a big grin on his face.

"Hey stranger, you look fantastic. The holiday with your parents must have been great".

"It was" I lied. "How is everything with you?".

"Fine, fine. How about a bottle of wine and pizza?" he said as he brought them out from behind his back.

"Sure, sounds great" I replied.

As we walked upstairs, I felt like I was in seventh heaven. Max had to stay on for a couple more days to sort out the new client base and ship things back. We had spent the last two days at the retreat, in bed, exploring each other's bodies. I couldn't imagine anything better than having Max moving inside me.

"I can't get over how much you have changed over the week. It's like you're a different person. Did something happen while you were away?" Mitch asked.

"No, nothing really. It was just great catching up with my parents and getting a tan in Italy. Maybe it is all that fresh European air" I said, feeling guilty for lying.

Mitch placed the bottle of wine down on the bench and grabbed out two glasses from the cabinet and poured us one each.

"Well, here's to your safe return and back to normality" he said.

I clinked my glass with his and then took a sip, it was delicious.

We sat down on the deck overlooking the ocean, ate pizza, laughed and drank two bottles of wine. I was not going to repeat my last mistake with the wine, so made sure I drank it slowly.

"So how about a movie tonight, are you up to it?" Mitch said.

"Sounds fantastic. I might just take a quick shower though and get the airport grit out of my hair, I will be out in about ten minutes. You can choose the movie while you wait if you like. I like most things, just not really romantic, sloppy movies. Okay?".

"Deal on that one" Mitch said, as he moved onto the couch and grabbed the television remotes.

As the water poured over my body and the soap suds clung to my breasts, I couldn't help wish that Max was here now. We hadn't explored each other in the shower yet, but it was something I had wanted to do.

I heard the bathroom door open and turned to see Mitch standing there naked in front of me. His erection evident.

He moved over and opened the door of the shower and walked me back towards the wall.

I didn't know what to do as part of me was thinking that this is something I had wanted for years, but the other part of me was telling me to stop now because of Max.

The wine was starting to have an effect and my body was betraying me. He moved his hands up to my face and brought it to his.

The kiss was nothing like Max's, but I felt the familiar flutter of the butterflies that I always had around Mitch.

The water lapped over us as he picked me up and pulled me down onto him. I gasped aloud as he moved me against the wall and thrust into me. One of his hands held me up while the other moved over my breasts and nipples.

I moaned aloud and found that he was already climaxing inside of me.

It hit me then. I had just cheated on Max and had waited years to find out that sex with Mitch was nothing compared to making love with Max.

"You have to leave" I said, my heart full of guilt for betraying Max. "I'm sorry but this was a mistake".

"What? Sarah, I thought you felt the same as I did" he said, looking hurt.

"I don't know what I feel anymore. I'm sorry, but can you please leave".

He grabbed his clothes, dressed quickly and I heard the door close behind him.

How would I ever tell Max? Did I have to tell him? Could I keep it a secret?

Whatever was to happen, I had only two days before Max would be turning up on my doorstep.

I only hoped that the man I now knew I loved, would understand.

Chapter 12

The knock at the door was something I had been waiting for, for the past two days.

I opened it to see Max, dressed in black dress pants and a blue business shirt. Even the sight of him made me weak at the knees. He walked in, dropped his bags down and closed the door behind him.

He moved quickly forward and placed his hands gently on my face and I could feel his warm breath against mine.

"I missed you so much, Sarah" he said, looking into my eyes.

I smiled and he kissed me deeply, not waiting for a reply.

Instantly, I felt that connection again and as our kisses became feverish. I could feel my heart beating rapidly in my chest.

He lifted me up and I wrapped my legs around him as he carried me into the lounge, and he sat down on the couch, so I was straddling him.

His tongue moved deeper into my mouth as his hands moved up my back. I unbuttoned the first button on his shirt and then ripped it open so that buttons flew off in all directions.

He laughed softly and deeply.

"It seems that you missed me too" he said, smiling.

I didn't answer him, instead I kissed him deeper, showing him how much I had missed him.

He moved my shirt up with his hands and then pulled it over my head, exposing my already erect nipples.

Placing his mouth on them and flicking the tip of his tongue over each one sent spasms down my body, and I could feel myself getting wetter.

He lifted me up and placed me on my back across the couch and pushed my short skirt up to my waist. I heard him moan at the surprise I had for him as I had no underwear on.

"Sarah, you turn me on so much" he whispered, his voice hoarse with emotion.

He lowered his head between my legs and licked my warm, wet lips. His tongue probed and flicked over my clitoris, and I moaned and arched my back with each delicious spasm. He darted his tongue inside me, and I felt the delicious hot, wet, liquid start to run down between my thighs.

He undid his belt and removed his pants quickly and as I looked at his fully erected manhood, I knew I wanted to take him in my mouth. Pushing him back against the couch, I moved down on my knees and looked him in the eyes before taking him into my welcoming mouth. Max uttered a guttural moan as I moved my lips up and down his thick, hard shaft. His taste was delicious, and I couldn't get enough and licked every escaping drop that I could from him. Feeling the head of his manhood pressing against the back of my throat was only making me wetter and I could feel the sensation of my own warmth building deep inside me.

"Sarah, I'm going to explode if you don't stop soon. I want to be inside you so badly" he said.

I smiled at him and licked him one last time, then stood up from the couch, took his hand and walked him into my bedroom. The room was full of sun and light and that was just how I wanted it. I wanted to make love with him in my room and be able to see every inch of his perfect body.

He pushed me playfully onto the covers and kissed me deeply as I placed my legs around him. His kisses were so passionate and the heat in our bodies melded together. I could feel the tip of his manhood pressing against my warm welcoming lips and as he pulled me down onto him, I cried out his name.

Max was hard, and the thickness of his penis spread me open so much that I didn't know if I could fully take him in.

He moved slowly in and out of me and I felt my body shiver all over. Kissing became slower and more sensual as our tongues danced together. I couldn't help but moan loudly with every movement.

Max moved his fingers gently over my clitoris and I knew that I was going to climax soon. Realising that we were both so close, his thrusts became more powerful, and I arched my back with each one, pushing my body against his so that his full length was filling me up. I watched the agony and ecstasy on his face as he was trying not to explode.

I kissed him deeper, our tongues moving together like we were magnets drawn to each other. I felt the familiar rush of warmth escape me and he gasped at the force of my climax, thrusting harder and faster into me. I gripped onto him as he climaxed and filled me with his hot wetness.

As I lay back in his arms, I couldn't help but feel emotional.

A tear slipped down my cheek and Max wiped it away.

"Did I hurt you, Sarah?" he said, concern in his voice.

"No" I smiled at him. "I have never felt so alive before and when you're inside me I just want it to be like this forever".

"I feel the same Sarah. For the past two days all I have wanted to do was get on the plane and come back to you. You possess my soul and my every waking thought. I love you Sarah".

Looking into his eyes, I brought my lips to his, kissing him softly.

"I love you to Max" I whispered in his ear.

We lay entwined together on the bed with the sheets twisted in a pile on the floor. I had never felt so happy and conflicted all at once.

I knew I should tell Max about the incident with Mitch, but I just couldn't. I loved Max and I couldn't bear to tell him what I had done for fear of losing him.

It had been a mistake. A stupid silly mistake, which I regretted. I had tried to contact Mitch to talk to him about it, but he had refused to speak to me.

Not knowing what else I could do about it, I decided to let Mitch cool down a bit before approaching him again.

For now, all I wanted to do was lie here in Max's arms and breath in his delicious scent.

Chapter 13

Being back at Elite felt fantastic. Dating Max had not only made me happier than I had ever been, but also more aware of the separation in my life of Sarah and Mistress Trix.

I had clients booked for the next week and had decided to stay at Max's apartment during the week so we could work together and at the end of the night we could rush home to his place and explore each other over and over again.

The girls at Elite were told about our relationship by Max and all of them were happy for us, apart from Mandy. She handed in her notice and left that day, which I couldn't blame her for as she always had a thing for Max and had slept with him once.

We had decided to spend weekends at my place so we could enjoy the ocean views and the beach right on our doorstep. As much as Max's apartment was closer to work, it was a typical males apartment filled with dark colours and large furniture and it wasn't my taste, but I stayed there to be with Max. not his interior.

The last semester of university had started, and I was glad that it would be over soon. Exams were coming up, so I reduced the days of working at Elite, but still spent time in the office studying. I did miss working and often sat in the viewing room watching the clients coming in for drinks. We had such a wide variety of clients from married men to single men (who could not hold down a normal relationship unless it involved BDSM), to virgins and old men who were firm believers in the little blue pill. All of them wealthy, but most of them somewhat lonely or conflicted in their day-to-day life.

Max had heard that the current owners were going to be listing Elite on the market soon and he discussed the idea to buy it from them, as he knew they would offer him a good rate as he had worked there for years.

I thought it was a fantastic idea and while I studied, Max spent his time in negotiations.

Tonight, I was booked with three clients, and I recognised their names all but one.

As my second client left and I had half an hour before the next client came in, I decided to go and sit in the viewing room.

I was dressed in my red leather catsuit tonight which came with another full head mask, and I realised that the more I wore the head masks, the more I felt powerful in them. The client could only see my lips, eyes and my hair, so it felt empowering to cover up the rest of my face so they would never know who was under it.

Max came into the room dressed all in black and I couldn't help but feel a deep sense of desire when I looked at him. It was amazing to me just how Max could instantly turn me on, and I often visualised ripping off his clothes and taking him in the viewing room.

He walked over and kissed me gently on the lips then took my hands and kissed both palms which made my body tingle.

"What are you doing in here, Sarah?".

"Just waiting for my last client. What are you doing in here, Max?".

"Looking for you, of course. Your client is running a little late. He rang and has requested something that I am not too happy with, but as you are the Mistress then I need to run it past you".

"Okay, what is it? I replied.

"He has asked to touch you while you are wearing clothing, on your breasts and buttocks only" Max said.

I looked at Max and could see he was very apprehensive about what I was going to say next.

"What do you think Max? What is your honest opinion, as the Manager of Elite?".

"That is a hard one to answer, Sarah. As a Manager, I allow you to do only so much, and that goes for the other girls too. There were some incidents with Mandy where she took the rules to the extreme and had sex with one of her clients and I had to reign her in on that. Other than that, one incident, I have never had to stop a session with anyone here. As Sarah there is no way that I want someone else touching the woman I love, but as Trix you seem to have a different air about you, and I have learnt to disconnect the two. Trix is a powerful dominatrix who punishes men but knows it's her job. Sarah is the woman who I make love to every day and every night and who possesses me with her mind, body and soul. Sarah is not here when you are working, Trix takes over and I have seen that".

"What about the fact that you didn't like the birthday boy touching me. How will you cope with someone else doing that?".

He sat back and I could see him thinking it through.

"Sarah, when I saw you and him together, it wasn't the fact that I thought you were going to get him off and give him the fantasy that he wanted. I was jealous because I knew you were enjoying it and part of me wondered if it was Trix enjoying it or Sarah. Trix is not the one I was falling for at that stage, it was Sarah and always has been Sarah.

I moved off the stool, stood in front of him, reached up and placrd my arms around his neck, pulling him down towards me.

"You are an incredible man, Max. I'm so thankful that you love me and that you are in this forever. Please don't ever stop loving me, because all I want on this earth is for you to love me, as Sarah".

He kissed me tenderly and I felt myself melt into him.

I stood back slightly and looked into his eyes.

"Let him have his wish. Trix can show him a good time and then Sarah can leave, take her boyfriend home and make love to him".

Max smiled and laughed.

"Sounds fantastic to me. Listen, I have an appointment with the owners now at their apartment so I will come back here and pick you up afterwards, okay?"

I nodded, kissed him again and made my way over to the door.

"I love you Sarah" Max said as I reached for the handle.

"I love you too Max, and just to let you know, so does Trix" I smiled then walked out the door.

Chapter 14

When I opened the door to my room, the client was standing naked with his own full mask on and a cock ring already in place. It made me feel a little uneasy.

"Hello, my name is Mistress Trix. I know you have requested a special treat tonight and I have given consent for you to touch my breasts and my buttocks. There will be no nudity on my side, of course, but I'm sure you will find the leather catsuit I am wearing will enhance the feel of everything. What you also must know is that the power to stop you touching me is in my hands, not yours. I have heard that you have been here before, so you know the rules and the word to use if you want to stop. Is there anything else you would like to ask or request?".

"Yes. I would like to have the same rules that applied last time, Mistress Trix".

I felt the air quickly leave my lungs as I recognised his voice, it was Mitch.

Thoughts of whether I should continue or if I should call an end to the session and give him to someone else, quickly played over my mind. As soon as I started thinking this, I relaxed a little, as I realised that he didn't know who I was under this suit. He knew me only as Mistress Trix! Tonight, I decided that he would get exactly that, Mistress Trix. I didn't need to feel ashamed anymore and I had put the night we had together behind me. Maybe this could make up for me hurting him too? Tonight, he could have Mistress Trix because he would never have Sarah again!

"Take your position by the wall. You should know the drill by now, birthday boy".

I chained his hands and feet and then brought out a whip I used on some of my clients. It was a little harder but didn't leave any marks on their backs when I whipped them with it.

Bringing the whip back and slashing him across his back, he yelled out and the chains shook as he tried to steady himself.

"Do you want it harder or softer?" I asked.

"Harder please, Mistress Trix" he replied.

I pulled my hand back and this time hit him over the buttock and thigh area. His knees buckled slightly, and his body quivered as I heard him breathing heavily through his mask.

"Did you like that birthday boy? Did it nearly make you spill on my floor?".

"Yes, Mistress Trix. Please can I have another?" he begged.

"Bend over with your head against the wall and I will give you something that you will enjoy".

He bent over and placed his head against the wall. I used the end of the whip to move his legs apart more so I could get to where I wanted to.

I stood back and angled the whip so that it would hit his buttock but would also move across his hardened member.

Taking my hand back, I swiftly brought it down across the buttocks and the tips of the leather whip hit his hard member in the correct place, making him orgasm and spill on the floor.

Looks like the drinks were on me tonight, I thought.

He bent over as a stream of hot liquid continued to course down him and onto the floor. I unfastened the chains, and he stood up and turned towards me. I moved forward and kissed him on the mouth and then allowed him to feel my backside while I moved my tongue further into his mouth.

Standing back, I could see that he was still slightly hard and decided that using the flogger whip would probably be the best item, as it was soft.

I walked him over to the pole in the middle of the room and tied his hands behind his back. This time he could watch what I was doing instead of being blind folded.

I draped the flogger over his chest and stomach and made sure the leather tentacles touched his member briefly.

He moaned through gritted teeth, and I couldn't help but feel that maybe he should find someone that was into this in his personal life. He had climaxed within only a few minutes when we were in the shower, but he seemed to stay harder when he was being whipped or flogged.

I made sure his eyes were looking at the flogger as I brought it down hard on to him. His knees bent and I knew he was probably having a hard time containing himself. I moved him back into standing position and then kissed him deeply. He moaned aloud as I moved my body down over his then turned around and moved my leather covered buttocks over his swollen hardness.

He cried out again as I moved away and brought the flogger back down onto him. This started a ritual of me flogging him, kissing him and then rubbing my body over his. After about ten minutes I could hear him being close to climaxing again, so I untied his hands, flogged him once more, kissed him again then moved my buttocks down over him. He pulled my body close to his and grabbed my breasts in his hands feeling the leather through his fingers. I bent over further and slide my backside up and slowly down over him as he held on to my hips and moaned. I pulled away quickly and felt my face exposed to the air.

I turned around, looked at him and saw he was holding my mask in his hand.

The look of shock on his face was all too evident. Now he knew my secret!

"Sarah? What the?" he said, looking at me.

I stood there for a second not knowing what to do. I felt angry that he had taken my mask away and I was now exposed.

"Please don't tell me that you are Mistress Trix!" he said.

I grabbed my head mask from him and pointed to the bathroom.

"Go and get dressed, then come back in here. I will discuss it with you after you have a shower".

He looked down at his engorged hardness and then walked over to the bathroom. I heard the taps go on and then heard him cry out as he took the cock ring off.

I took off my gloves, tied my hair back again, then thought about what I needed to say.

He walked back in the room after about ten minutes and stood by the restraints table dressed in a pair of dark jeans, blue shirt and black shoes.

"Tell me the truth, are you Mistress Trix and if so, how long have you been doing this for?".

I told him everything apart from the bit about Max. He didn't need to know about him. Max was not part of my Mistress Trix life.

"So, this whole time you've known it was me, but you never told me. Even when you must have known I had feelings for you. You had sex with me at your house when you returned from your holiday and then basically decided to ignore my feelings for you. It's all so messed up Sarah!".

"It's not messed up, Mitch. I have had feelings for you since I was in junior high, but you never once looked at me. I wanted to be your girlfriend so badly at times, but you were always dating the pretty blondes, so I knew there was no hope for me as Sarah. When I found out about this line of work, I was so attracted to it and knew I could be good at it, if not great. When you came here on your birthday, I still had a crush on you, and it was like my fantasies had all come true. With getting to know you outside of here, I still didn't know whether you preferred me as Sarah or as Trix. It was confusing to me how you could come here and be hard and last for a long time, but when we were in the shower that one time it was completely different. We just didn't have that chemistry anymore when I was Sarah, only when I was Trix. That's when I knew that we couldn't be together. I'm so sorry that you had to find out this way, but my life here is very important to me as I'm free from the girl I am at university. I'm really sorry that I didn't tell you and that it didn't work out with us. All I ask is that you please keep this a secret".

He looked at me, then placed his hands in his pockets.

"I thought you would be more understanding of that episode in the shower. Yes, what I have with Trix blows my mind and even I can't figure out how I can be so aroused and last for a long time with her but can't hold my load when having sex with what I thought was a normal girl".

As soon as he said it, I knew that he regretted it.

"I am a normal girl in every way. I just like to use whips and chains on men sometimes so they can feel good about themselves too. This is why I didn't stop and place you with anyone else tonight, as I felt I needed to say sorry about what happened at my apartment, and this was the only way I knew how".

His face was red with embarrassment, and I could see how upset he was. I felt terrible.

"Apology accepted" he said as he walked past me and walked out the door.

I sat back down and heard the door open again. Thinking that he must have forgotten something I looked up and saw Max standing there instead.

From the look on his face, I could tell he had been watching me and had obviously heard everything.

"Is it true? Did you sleep with him after you and I had spent the week together?"

I looked at him as tears welled up in my eyes and then nodded my head.

He looked at me, shook his head slightly and turned to walk out the door. I ran for the door and shut it before he could exit.

"Please, please listen to what I have to say before you walk out that door".

He looked at me, the emotions on his face so raw. He nodded and took a step away from me.

"I came back from the week with you so happy and Mitch was waiting at my place with wine and pizza. I had a bottle of wine then said I had to take a shower. The next thing I know he is naked in the shower with me and is kissing me. Yes, I completely messed up and did the worst thing I can possibly think of, but I realised that it was a mistake and I asked him to leave. I was so confused as to whether the boy I had fantasised about for years was all that my mind had imaged it to be, or whether the man I was falling in love with was what I needed. I haven't seen him again until tonight, although I tried to contact him a couple of times just to apologise. Don't you understand that when it happened my first thought was about how I wanted to be with you and only you".

Max looked at my eyes and I could see he was hurt and angry.

"When you had sex with him where you Sarah or Trix?".

I looked at the floor and then back up at him with tears falling down my cheeks.

"I had sex with him as Sarah, the girl who had some stupid fantasy for years about him. I regretted it straight away and was so scared to tell you in case you would leave me. I don't know what I would do without you Max, you are my life".

Max looked at my lips and up to my eyes, then stepped forward and kissed me. I wasn't expecting it, but I was so happy.

He then took my head gently in his hands and moved his mouth just above my ear and kissed the side of my head.

"Goodbye Sarah, I really hope you find what you're looking for".

I gasped and stumbled as he moved around me and opened the door.

Screaming out after him, I ran down the corridor and tried to get him to stop but he wouldn't. I stood there in the middle of the hallway and cried desperately as Max walked out the door.

A few of the girls came out of their rooms to see what was going on and a couple of them came over to wrap me in their arms.

I couldn't comprehend what had just happened, but I knew I had to fight to get him back.

I asked Kittie to lock up and made my way to the changing rooms where I took off my makeup and dressed into my normal clothes.

I grabbed my bag and took off in my car towards Max's place. When I arrived, I could see that his apartment had no lights on, so I made my way inside using the spare key Max had given me. There were clothes spread all over the floor in his bedroom and his suitcases were missing, along with his toiletries. I sunk down on the floor as the realisation that he had left came over me.

How could I be so stupid not to tell him straight away when it had happened? Would it have changed the outcome, or would it have ended up just the same?

I couldn't stay here tonight as I felt I was invading his space and I couldn't lie in his bed breathing in his scent without him being there next to me.

I gathered my things and walked back down to the car.

When I arrived home, I felt somewhat comforted in my apartment by the sea and opened the doors to let the ocean air fill my lungs.

Sleep was not something that I wanted. I couldn't bear going to sleep without Max's arms around me and spent the night crying and leaving messages on his phone. I couldn't live my life without Max, because Max was my life.

When the phone rang the next morning, I was surprised to find it was the owner of Elite on the other end. He informed me that Max had handed in his notice and would not be returning to Elite. He then offered me Max's position at Elite, as they had watched my work and had heard from the girls working there that they would be happy working under me if given the opportunity.

I thanked him for his offer but said I needed some time to think it over. He gave me three days to think about it, then would need my answer.

At that moment I just wanted to get off the phone and break down. Max had left and he wasn't coming back, my heart was breaking knowing I would never see him again.

It was all my fault.

Chapter 15

Life without Max was unbearable. Everywhere I turned I thought I saw him, but it was always someone else.

After returning to university and seeing the gossips making their rounds, mostly everyone who knew Mitch. It seemed he had got his revenge and had told anyone he could about my new occupation.

My friends were great and stood by me. They all joked about the law job, and I told them about everything, about Mitch and Max and also the offer I was made by the owners of Elite.

They all thought it was a great idea, not to mention the pay and responsibilities that came with it.

I didn't care about the pay. I would give it all up if Max walked back in the door.

As the weeks went by, I realised that he was never coming back, and I decided to take the job at Elite. I confessed to my parents about what I was doing, as they were bound to find out. Funny enough they said they were happy, if I was happy and never berated me about my role as Mistress Trix. They thought it was ingenious and a much more interesting job than being a lawyer. I couldn't love them any more for saying that to me and for once I felt like I was their daughter.

A new life started for me in a way. I still had Mistress Trix, although she was retired from seeing clients, she became the new Manager of Elite.

After three months of putting myself and everything into my new role, I was advised by the owners that the premises had been sold and would be undergoing major renovations by the new owner. We were told our jobs were secure and that only the interior would be changed and the name. The new name was Morph, which was obviously in reference to the caterpillar into a butterfly effect that many people felt at our premises. I think it fit in very well with what was happening.

It took two months to renovate the whole place and when it was finished it was beautiful. The new interiors were soft whites, warm greys, black and copper. The furnishings were ultra-modern and sophisticated. It reminded me of a very updated Art Deco inspired establishment that celebrities would flock to. The clientele was still only the very wealthy and although we lost a few who did not like the new look, we gained so many younger clients that didn't like the dark and slightly seedy look of Elite.

Business was so busy that I had to hire more staff and I brought in some new fresh-faced girls who were a hit with the customers.

We had a grand opening celebration which was set in a 1940s Gatsby theme. We hired ceiling ribbon acrobats who wore white and black bondage outfits, and the place was filled with clients. Champagne was flowing and the men were dressed in black tie with the girls dressed in slinky cocktail dresses, stiletto heels and diamond head jewellery.

I grabbed a bottle of champagne and left Kittie in charge, then walked back to my office to finish up the book work.

As I opened the door, I nearly dropped the bottle as I saw Max sitting in my chair.

"Hello Sarah" he said.

I placed the bottle down on the table then stood there looking at him, wondering if I was dreaming.

"Max, is it really you?" I said, my voice shaking.

He stood up and came towards me.

"Sarah, I want you to listen to me and not say a word until I have finished, can you do that?".

I nodded, not willing to reply, wanting instead to listen.

"I was such a fool to leave you, Sarah. I didn't give you a chance really and I also didn't listen to what you had to say. If I had listened, then I would have heard you when you explained what happened with

Mitch and that it was different to what we had together. I didn't hear you when you told me you loved me because I was hurt. I think I needed the time away to understand why you did it and to understand that you had already made the conscious decision that you wanted me and not Mitch. It hurt me so much when you told me that it was Sarah who had sex with him and not Trix. Sarah is the woman I love, and I couldn't bear to think of anyone else touching you and especially not having sex with you. I left you and in doing so I left you alone with the guilt and pain, for that I'm so sorry".

Tears started to flow down my cheeks as I couldn't contain my happiness that he was back.

"I'm so sorry Max, I wish it had never happened, but it did. I never wanted to hurt you, I just wanted to forget it had ever happened so that I could continue being the woman that you loved, not the stupid girl. I love you so much Max. My life is not the same if you're not in it".

He came towards me and kissed my face gently where my tears had fallen, then kissed me deeply. The fire ignited within my belly, and I could feel myself melt into him. Our hands moved over each other's bodies as we frantically took off each other's clothes. Standing naked in front of him I felt all the sorrow lift away from me and as I reached out and placed my fingers around his hardness. I knew I couldn't wait to have him inside me.

He cleared the top of the desk in one movement and then lay me down on top of it. He kissed me deeply and moved down my body, kissing every inch that he could. When he plunged his tongue deep inside my warmth, I couldn't help but moan at the pure pleasure. He flicked his tongue over me, inside of me, sending pleasurable shocks through my body. I tried hard not to explode.

Twisting and turning, plunging so deep that his face pressed hard against me, I felt the familiar sensation in my stomach and then the explosion between my thighs as he lapped up my juice with his mouth.

He stood up and moved my legs onto his chest and I could feel the tip of his hardness entering me. Max moaned with pleasure as he thrust deep into me and I held onto the top of the desk and pushed myself against him with each thrust, crying out as he moved deep within me.

As he placed his hands around my hips, pulling me harder and harder towards him with each thrust I knew he was getting close, but I wanted it to be me giving him the pleasure.

I moved him out of me then sat him in my chair. I sat with my back towards him, placed both feet inside of his and lowered myself onto his thick shaft. His hands cupped my breasts as I moved up and down over his hardness. I heard him groan behind me as I moved faster, harder.

"Oh Sarah, you're amazing" he whispered.

I moved myself up and down on him faster and harder while he held onto my hips and helped thrust deeper into me. I could feel him thicken and knew he was so close to exploding.

I moved off him and got down on my knees. This is what I had wanted for so long. I wanted him to explode in my mouth.

Taking him into my mouth he put his head back and moaned. I moved my mouth up and down his shaft and then took his full length in me so that I could feel it pressing into the back of my throat.

Moving swiftly up and down, sucking and swallowing any little drops, I felt him thrusting deeper as he moved my head down onto him swift and fast. He moaned loudly and with one last deep thrust he spilled into me.

I swallowed his warm juices, licked and savoured every last drop that I could of his delicious taste.

He pulled me up onto the chair and wrapped his arms around me the kissed me with such longing.

When we looked at each other, we were both out of breath.

"Sarah, I had dreamed of this for the past few months and I'm sorry it took me so long to get out of my own head. Please forgive me" he said, emotion in his voice.

I kissed him gently on the lips and placed my head against his shoulder.

"It's me that needs to ask for forgiveness, Max. I should never have done what I did. Please forgive the messed-up schoolgirl that I once was".

"There is nothing to forgive. I want to be with you forever Sarah and I never want to spend another night away from you again. Sarah, I want us to live together so that we can keep exploring each other and loving each other for the rest of our lives".

Tears welled up in my eyes as I had never felt so happy.

We walked together into the shower where Max erased every thought of Mitch away. He made love to me with so much passion and love that I felt myself becoming the woman I had always dreamed I could be.

The party was in full swing downstairs and Max, and I stayed close to each other all night like magnets. When it ended, the clean-up crew came in and we drove home to my place.

As we entered and opened up the doors to let the ocean breeze in, I closed my eyes and felt his arms come around me.

"Sarah, I think we should live out here by the ocean. There's something here that makes you light up and I want to be a part of that. We could make this our temporary base until we buy our own house by the sea. I want to be able to have something of our own that we can eventually raise our children in.

As I felt his hands move away from me, I opened my eyes and turned to see Max down on one knee.

"Sarah, I love you beyond anything I could ever have imagined, and I want to spend the rest of my life making love with you, laughing with you and one day making our children with you. You're my life just as much as I am yours, will you please do me the honour of becoming my wife".

He opened a beautiful small box in his hand, and I saw the shine of the diamonds twinkle in the reflection of the moonlit sky.

"Yes, Max yes! A million times, yes!" I said as he placed the ring on my finger.

He pulled me into his arms, and we kissed.

Chapter 16

In the morning we drove back to Morph, both slightly exhausted from our night of love making. The ring sparkled on my finger and when I told my parents the news and Max spoke to them about our plans, we agreed to fly over to Italy in a few weeks so they could meet him in person and plan the wedding.

My mother wept happily down the phone, and I knew she would be busy calling around for the best wedding planner she could find. We had decided to get married quickly as we both agreed that we didn't want to waste any further time.

As we pulled up to Morph, I saw a familiar blue mustang parked outside and watched as Mitch got out.

"What is he doing here?" I spoke.

"It's alright, I rang him and asked him to come over. I think it's time you two cleared the air. I think you also might know a solution to his little issue as well. Someone we have working here that may be perfect for him, someone blonde and petite" he said winking at me.

I knew straight away who he meant, and I smiled. Mistress Candy was very cute, the same age as Mitch and was also from a wealthy family who never understood her. She had her own place and not only liked whips and chains at work, but also at home. She was very kind-hearted, and I knew she desperately wanted to meet someone. They were perfect for each other!

As Max walked over to the door and opened it with his own cardkey, I looked on puzzled. He laughed, came towards me and kissed me.

"Well, I do own Morph you know" he said.

"No, I didn't know that thanks for telling me" I said, laughing and kissing him back.

"Well, it's not like we actually had much time to talk last night" he whispered.

He kissed my neck playfully and walked inside.

Mitch walked over to me, and I could see he was nervous.

"Let's go get a drink inside and sit down, it's too hot out here" I said blushing slightly.

He nodded and we walked up the stairs to the lounge bar. Max already had a bottle of champagne chilling in ice, so I popped it open and poured us two glasses.

We sat down and Mitch took off his jacket, placing it next to him.

"Max was good to ring me as I really didn't know how to approach this, Sarah. I'm so sorry about what I did at uni and how I told everyone. That was totally insensitive, and I did it because I was confused and hurt. I thought about what you said and you're correct. If I'm being honest with you, I knew that you had feelings for me at school, but I was not interested because I was shallow, and you didn't turn me on. When I came to Elite, I mean Morph, I was blown away by how Mistress Trix made me feel. In all honesty it was the power you had and the equipment that I liked. Finding out that you were Sarah underneath changed my mind about Mistress Trix. Sarah is this lovely girl who I connected with on a friend level and when we had sex in the shower, I also didn't feel that connection and therefore that is probably why I lost myself fast. I just didn't really understand that fully until you pointed it out. I'm sorry that I made you feel bad about what happened between us, and I should never have walked into your shower and come onto you. But then again, looking back at it, maybe if I didn't then you also wouldn't have fully realised what you had with Max, and from what I can see it's something very special".

I moved my hand in front of him so he could see my engagement ring.

"Okay, wow. So yeah, something much more than just special. Congrats".

"Yes, Mitch you're right. I love Max completely, which is why I have agreed to marry him and retire Mistress Trix, forever. I'm glad you came here today so we could clear the air and hopefully we can remain friends. I forgive you for telling everyone, but in a funny way you actually freed me from keeping it a secret. I know how it must feel not being able to get that aspect of what you found pleasurable with Mistress Trix into your dating life, but I might be able to help you there" I said, then turned and looked at the viewing room window and nodded, knowing Max was there watching us.

The door to the bar opened and Mistress Candy walked in. She had a short leather pink skirt on with a ruffled petticoat underneath which came up so high that you could see her pert, tight buttocks underneath. Her shirt was white and was tied off under her breasts, which were a good size but obviously enhanced. She wasn't wearing a bra so you could see her nipples clinging through the shirt material. Her thighs were bronzed, and she wore pink stilettos with little candy pieces printed on top, her blonde hair was tied up into a ponytail and her blue eyes shone through the pink eye mask she was wearing.

I could see his excitement straight away and knew that this match was good, very good.

Moving forward I whispered into his ear.

"This is Mistress Candy. She is the same age as you and doesn't attend our university. She comes from a very wealthy family but is like us, a free agent to do what she pleases. She's also very single and looking for someone that she can give great pleasure to. She loves whips and chains both here and at home and I think you would be perfect together".

Mistress Candy walked over to Mitch and held out her hand.

"I have been informed of your terms and I agree to them all. Would you like to come with me Birthday Boy" she said, licking her smooth pink lips.

Mitch stood up and took her hand, then he smiled at me and mouthed 'thank you'.

Max was in the viewing room when I entered and was smiling.

"Okay, so what did you tell Candy about the terms?"

I walked up to him as he took me in his arms and then pulled me into him so I could feel his arousal pressing against me.

"I told her that he likes to kiss passionately between each punishment. That he likes the bull whip and the flogger. I also told her that he is single and looking for a long-term relationship with someone that likes to use equipment at home too. I also said that as she is not really on the clock yet and we don't open for another two hours, to do whatever she wanted to do in that time, and she wouldn't be reprimanded for it" he said looking very sheepish.

"Does that mean sex?" I spoke.

"Well let's just say this, when she saw, him sitting talking to you, she asked how far she could take it and I asked her what she meant. Turns out that she has seen him around as they move in the same social circle. She has always wanted to talk to him but has been too shy. When she saw him tonight and I told her about how aroused he gets here, she asked me straight out whether she could go as far as she wanted to with him, if he wanted to. So, I agreed. Maybe Mitch will get everything he wanted and more".

I looked at Max and knew he was right. We didn't allow the girls to have go all the way with the clients, but maybe just this once we could let Mitch and Candy find out just how good they could be together.

Max kissed me as I moved my hand over him and pulled down the zip of his pants.

"What are you doing Sarah? He said, his voice hoarse.

"Well as you said we are not open for another two hours, so maybe we should make the most of that time and christen the viewing room".

He grinned then moved my skirt up over my thighs exposing my naked backside. He moved his hands down and grasped my buttocks in his hands. He lifted me up onto the table as I lifted his shirt up over his head. He slid his hand between my thighs and felt the warmth between my legs as his fingers entered me.

I moaned as he thrust deeper into me, and I realised this is what my life was going to be. A life full of desire.

Mistress Trix would always be a part of me, but Sarah was now in charge.

As Max thrust into me sending me into climax, I knew that he was the only man I would ever want.

My story as Mistress Trix was ending, but I knew that somewhere in Morph a new one was just beginning.

The story of Mistress Candy.

THE END

** if you enjoyed this book, please keep a look out for my next one titled 'My secret life as a High School Dominatrix – Mistress Candy'.

9 798223 527428